T.M. Cooks is the pen name ___ ___
laborative writing team. The contributors are:

- Ashley Pattison

- Alice Broad

- Jordan White

- Morgan Warrilow

- Joe Hill

- Mitchell Powell

- Emma Williams

- Kyran Phokeerdoss

with cover design by Joe Hill. The project was overseen by Joe Reddington, Dr Yvonne Skipper and Richard Seymour.

The group cheerfully acknowledges the wonderful help given by:

- Ruby-Leigh Tonks

- Stephanie Sale

- Mick Sturland

- The Keele University school of Psychology for coming to our rescue

And a big thank you goes to White Water Writers who funded this wonderful project.

It's been a wonderful opportunity, and everyone involved has been filled with incredible knowledge and enthusiasm.

Finally, we would like to thank all staff at Newfriars College Project Search for their support in releasing our novelists from lessons for a full week.

The group started to plan out their novel at 9.15 on Monday 17th December 2018 and completed their last proof reading at 13.40 on Friday 21st December 2018.

We are incredibly proud to state that every word of the story, every idea, every chapter and yes, every mistake, is entirely their own work. No teachers, parents or other students touched a single key during this process, and we would ask readers to keep this in mind.

We are sure you will agree that this is an incredible achievement. It has been a true delight and privilege to see this group of young people turn into professional novelists in front of our very eyes.

The Lake of Secrets

T. M. Cooks

Contents

Chapter 1

Folk Lore

A group of people were in a room in the town hall, and Bella was in the meeting. Bella and the people were talking amongst themselves about the strange, suspicious feelings they had been having. Bella started to explain, but suddenly stopped herself.

Adele started to walk the lake slowly and she had a sandwich on this plate. Adele went to the shack house to dropped off the sandwich and walked away from the shack on the lake. Adele started to walk towards back to the bakery.

Adele walked back to the bakery and talked to Bella. Adele is the mother of Bella. She told her daughter Bella that she had made a secret recipe. The secret recipe was for a special sandwich. Bella wondered what the secret was in the sandwich. She found out, and told the whole town about it. The people started to tell everyone else, and before long, everyone found out.

Chapter 2

The Great Sacrifice: Part 1

Inside the woods it was crusty-snow covered, misty, soggy and was surrounded by colourful leaves which were gradually falling off the trees. Bella's Mum called Adele is being suspiciously, secretive and creates the sandwich which is a magical, powerful possession to her. Bella's Mum doesn't want anybody to find out about the secret of the sandwich. Bella's Mum is in a mysterious, spooky, wondrous woods and is making a sandwich which has got suspicious ingredients in. She has got a warm, comfy jumper on, with

. Bella's mum sacrificed herself to hell when Bella was 18 years old. This means she gave up something important, gave up freedom, independence, her possession of the suspicious sandwich, family and friends. The reason why she did this is because she thought it will help with something more important such as saving the world, protecting her family and friends and keeping everyone safe and secure.

Bella becomes the guardian and her Mum told her not to mention to anybody about the sandwich as it would have bad side effects and could possibly kill you. It was Bella's job of

protecting and defending everything which was taking place around the sandwich.

Bella wants to get the police to get the detectives on her side so they believe and will be very understanding. Bella's Mum wants to do an investigation on finding her other sisters as she doesn't know where they have disappeared. Mum desperately needs to get out of hell as it's dark and dull there.

Bella and Ms Evans had a private conversation so Ms Evans would be extremely understanding of Bella's side of the story.

Ms Evans will be super sympathetic. Before Adele went into hell she whispered into Bella's ear saying "I love you and don't worry I will be okay! "

Chapter 3

Riot

It was half past 6 in the morning when James got up from a nightmare. He screamed then it took him a couple of seconds to realise why he was sweating with exhaustion, trying to catch his

breath, remembering the time when he was at Iraq fighting, running, getting in cover, watching people getting killed right in front of him. Seeing his friends die all around him, killing the people who killed his brothers in arms and remembering the person who sliced half his face between the eyes and on the right side of his mouth.

He decided to get up and have a quick wash. After that he looked at himself in the reflection of the mirror seeing his both sides of his head cut clean while the top of his head is curved to one side. He was still looking at the scar on his head. It still stung when touched it. After a quick wash he puts on his police uniform, grabs some coffee and drove to the shops to get some bacon and cheese turnover for breakfast. James got to the police station while having his yummy breakfast. He entered the front entrance, someone noticed him and came up to him and said "Oh hey James uh we're getting some phone calls about a shack coming out of.."

"No, I haven't got time to listen to kids prank calls. You, Dave, we've got more pressing matters to attend to" said James, looking annoyed by this. "But there aren't any kids calling, there have been multiple reports of a shack coming out nowhere", said Dave with a nervous look on his face while struggling to catch up.

The police guarded the lake from the people who were gathering around the lake and wondering what has happened and more people then gathered. Then the police had to tell the people to get back more so the police had space to investigate it. More police arrived to help out the other police-man and women so it was easier for the police to control.

Chapter 4

Demon Detectives

The detectives turn up in a flashing car and tell everyone to leave the scene.

They order the police to keep the public back, so they don't mess with the evidence and hurt themselves by tripping in the lake, because they don't know what's in the lake yet. James comes over to John and says "Do you want me to look for witnesses to help us out, or not ?"

The police are a little bit lost for words, because they don't know what to do. They tell their boss there's nothing for them to do, but actually there is; they get some evidence from the lake to actually see what's there and to get into a deeper investigation with the lake. Even though the detectives are taking over in some way, there is still work for the police to do behind the scenes.

"Maybe you guys can help the detectives to find any clues around the shack, or in the shack, but in my opinion I don't think that it's a good idea for anyone to go in the shack for the moment. I think that you police officers should ask the public to see if they know anything about the day before it happened and I, as a most skilled detective, don't think that the townsfolk will forget this day for a long time!" said James.

James and the detectives agree with the fact that they should put up a curtain around the shack- "It's only because we don't want the public to be even more nosey."

As they put up the curtain the police and the detectives hear groans from the townsfolk who have gathered around to see what's happening with the shack. They want to know more information about it but unfortunately the police don't want to give too much away to the public. Not just yet.

The detectives and the police say that it's not just the right time to explain everything to the public. It's the right thing to do for Bella and her family to have time, to give respect to Bella in some way because she just lost her mother and her sisters .

James and the detectives have an argument about why the detectives are here and James starts to shout (so the whole town hears "What are you doing in my town, because I am the Sheriff of this town and what I says goes, do you understand me?". Then the detectives start to say "We have been sent from the government and what I mean by that, is that we've been sent by the Prime Minister of England!"

James storms off to his boss and the detectives were thinking to themselves "Goodbye and even though you're the Sheriff, we're from the government and basically the Prime Minister is saying you're rubbish and we're better than you!"

Chapter 5

A Small Conspiracy

After the towns commotion was calmed, three friends stop at a bakery cafe to have private conversation about why there is a shack on there. The lake. Unexpected detectives took control of the situation. The three friends were so attracted by the superb, sensational, spectacular smell of the delicious, delightful sense of food. They all had an extreme temptation of going into the bakery cafe as they thought it was luscious, luxurious and heavenly. They all felt so curious and inquisitive! They decided to do some problem solving to decide why there is a shack on the lake. It seems random and unusual that this would be true.

Three of them were figuring out what made the blackout happen and why there is a shack that suddenly appeared at first light of dawn. These three were always causing trouble that the townspeople were having so many problems. Despite what went down last night. They do begin to feel some guilt or responsibility towards it.

One of them even suggested to report themselves if it was the case but still itching at their skulls, remembering for what real reasons. Honestly they were there that night when the blackout started and mentioning of the shack sighting but not knowing of it's origin. So at the time they've broke in the arcade to cheat using tokens, this energy coming from the shack has increased and was overwhelmed that it caused a massive electrical shutdown in the town.

Whatever cause it seems unnatural for anyone else in town to be at fault and they were the

only ones at night to witness. Someone is still hiding from the town they thought and when it comes mind the one person to be more of a suspect is Athol. Only known as the old merchant who lives near the lake has been acting more different than usual. Since the shack appeared and was strangely attracted to it more than we did, he is the oldest person that lived even longer before their parents did. For now that's their objective, to try speaking with him and finding information on his secret obsession with the shack.

In the middle of all this bella who happens to work at the bakery overhears their plan and this is interesting but worried for what they might get into. This is because she knows what they're like and could get into serious trouble. Wondering how serious this could get, she thinks of the father who left her with a baker family as a child because of her mother's death. One day she hopes to return home when he comes to terms with his grief and shares his life with Bella once more.

Chapter 6

The Demon Returns

Jimmy goes to the shack. As he walks

to the shack he needs to be careful because he can get court. What he's doing is called trespassing. So Jimmy sneaks around the lake to get to the shack making funny noises as he walks giggling to what noises he's doing. He suddenly stops and says to himself "why am I being like a child for I need to take this series" then he slaps himself in the face to help him snap out of it and the he continues to find this shack. A couple of hours later he finds the shack and tries to find a way to get in.

Jimmy finds a way inside the shack. He sees a strange looking sandwich and starts to think what it can do so Jimmy looks at the sandwich. Jimmy says to himself "I need tell the demons and devils about this strange object maybe we can convince the humans to go to it". The great devil opens the portal.

"Since the demons and devils gave me this power I need to be careful in where I open this portal and check my surroundings too". As he goes through the portal spinning around in the portal he's singing then turns into a scream. He gets in. The hell portal opens up on the ceiling he doesn't realise so he hits the floor still screaming the demons are talking to each other. Demon 1 says "well we all go through terrible things like breaking up with a love one but we have no love ones we are just monsters ugly demons and devils. Now I think about it I hate being a demon and being in hell I want to be human again. that was amazing I had everything". Demon 2 Says "HEY! shut up moaning the more you moan about your life makes us not want to be here anymore. We love it here it's amazing but if you don't want be here anymore you can go to prison and stay in there forever. Demon 3 says "by the way the great devil is still screaming well you all of you are moaning about stuff that doesn't matter but I get demon 2 he's right so go to prison before we get father to take you by your rotting skull and bones well you cry about what you said and you regret what you said. And you can think about it as well if you have time to do that before you get your rotting body torn apart in a matter of seconds. "Oh no demon 2 says "you have done it now father is very angry and I don't think anyone wants to see father angry and upset everyone close your eyes and ears and scream so you don't hear father". demon 1 looks around and sees a big dark shadow over him he slowly turns around as he turns around faither dribbles all over him and looks down father says "you have been very ungrateful for what you have so your not going prison" demon 1 says "oh thank you father". Father says "oh right you didn't let me finish my sentence" demon 1 says "oh no im really sorry father please forgive me for what I said I don't mean it" father screams at him fathers scream is that loud it's louder than anything ever demon 1s head explodes and his body drops onto the floor. Father commands someone take this corpse out of my site demon 2 and 3. Father says "take it to the prison for the prisoners to eat" as demon 2 and 3 take the corpse they speak to one another demon 2 says to demon 3 "well he got what he deserved he should have let father finish his sentence" demon 3 "says to right"

Demon 3 says "hey stop screaming silly" the great devil stops and says "I totally wasn't screaming looks away looking like a fool but laughing in his head. The great devil says "But anyway what was I doing oh yes that's why I came down here because one of the demons said there was a strange creature around lurking he says he thinks it's lost go find it".

Chapter 7

Nothing Is Real

In hell it's just uncomfortable, different and scary. It's silent, creepy when the demons and devils creeply walk around. You can even hear their claws against the floor scratching, leaving marks all over the floor and walls. It's very hot but the demons love it and the devils do too. You may think they will hurt you but some won't and some will so be careful what you do and say to them because they can form into human on earth but when they are in hell they are devils and demons. It's creepy the fact that they look at you with a creepy grin it's like a smile but the sort of smile they are staring into your soul with glowing red eyes and dribbling. They have scars on their mouth where they tried to close their mouths but can't because of their sharp teeth. They bleed all the time in their mouth when you walk around hell. You can discover new places that are more creepier than anything. If you discover more into hell you might meet Satan, our father, he's the scariest. The great devil has to say a strange noise to open the portal to go back as Jimmy. If he wants to go back in hell he will do the same thing again by doing a strange noise. When the great devil does this other people around him can hear it but their eyes tend to bleed because it can affect others because they are not a devil, they are human.

It's constantly dark and silent in hell. Through hell the great devil is walking around and suddenly he can hear a demon crying saying things over and over again, saying "nothing nothing, i have is real. It's cold and dark down here, just nothing" as the demon says this he's shaking, twitching. All of the demons and devils are starting to think that there's something wrong like something is really wrong. They say to each other something is going to happen bad. The demons and devils are talking about this sandwich, laughing about it.

The great devil has found that creature he was on about, sees it and walks up to it and talks to the creature. He asks for its name. He says "Rock" the great devil says "I've never seen you around here before let me give you a tour around hell let's start off with Devils hotel. It is just normal hotel like on earth, but it's slightly different without colors it's just dark and spooky in all the rooms and corridors. As you walk down the corridors, you can hear their claws dragging across the floors. Now we will go to The devils corvery. Now that's a place for actual devils and demons. No humans are meant to be in there, well only some parts if you know what i mean haha. Now moving on".

"Well Rock, last place now, the prison. This is where all the bad devils and demons go. Now Rock believe me and trust me, you don't want go in there because you won't last for a couple of seconds. They eat each other and screaming crying and other things that you won't imagine them noises that were possible to do in the whole universe".

"Ah yes this is a human from earth she's been down here for 10 years somehow she is still alive, but we think she's lost her hearing because of the noises and screaming Every day and night she tries to cry but there's no tears left.

Chapter 8

The Unimaginable

Davide was sitting in his hotel room in France and sitting down having his dinner what was pasta what is his favourite food in the world. Davide was wearing his green suit with green socks and shoes all looking smart and smells very nice. Davide just turned on the tv and watching the news until he notice his old town was on it and spotted it was a blackout. David was feeling worried about his daughter he haven't seen in 5 years.

Meanwhile Davide was thinking about going back because he wanted to make sure if his daughter is ok and was getting upset about it and crying about it. Davide was about to go bed because it was pretty late but he could not as he was still worrying about his daughter Bella. Davide didn't get much sleep as he was getting up in the night and thinking about Bella and hoping she was ok.

The next day Davide woke up and was

still upset about his daughter Bella. When Davide was at

work he was still thinking about his daughter and thinking if she should go back or not. When Davide got back in his hotel about 8pm at night time and Davide sat down and relaxed Davide had his tea and it was pasta. Davide started thinking about his daughter Bella again.

Davide got up one morning was thinking again about his daughter Bella and He decided to ask work, if he can a couple of weeks of because of seeing his daughter who might in trouble in England. The work people who Davide works with say yes no problem at all. Davide was happy so he can see her daughter who he haven't seen in 5 years.

Davide went back to his hotel room in

France and Davide was packing all his bags to get back to England. Davide spent a few hours booking his fight from France - England and finishing off packing about 11pm then he got his hire car was a Ferrari 458 and he drove as fast as he could to Nice airport in south of France. Davide arrived at Nice airport at 4am and got on his own jet and took off around 4.30am. Davide had a rest on this flight was about 3hr 30mins and he arrived at Manchester Airport at 8am and Davide was feeling quite nervous about seeing his daughter after he haven't seen her for 5 years.

Chapter 9

A House Call

The group decide to sneak into Athol's house to find what was hidden, so they wait until dark because it's the more quiet approach. The group approach Athol's house slowly and steadily and made sure they go in quietly and don't make too much noise and not to wake up the rest of the town, (because the group might get into trouble).

Inside his house they managed to find nothing out of the ordinary, except for a secret room containing strange religious artifacts, ancient weapons and books lying around. They were out of words for this is not what they expected to find, making them too confused! The group had been searching for a while now and found nothing really bad, but when they went into the next room they find something.

In the middle of their shocked reactions, Athol surprises them and demands to know why they're in his house and looking through his private things. The group found some things in his room, but there was nothing to hide or anything to be suspicious about Athol.

They tried explaining to Athol the reason that they broke in, but also asked him about his possible connections to the mysterious shack on the lake and what caused the blackout. Athol replied to the group, explaining he wasn't the person who did this and had nothing to do with this. After a couple of minutes he told the group something else...

Out of their determination, Athol calmly confesses his knowledge about the events of the blackout and him knowing all along of the shacks existence. No one knew of its whereabouts but him, although it has always been on the lake since even before he moved here (which was a long time ago). Athol said that someone else could be involved in this and the group asked "Who?"

Athol replied, saying "Someone who is evil, or someone we don't know."

As everyone sits with him listening to why he's kept himself from the town, he talks about his history with the supernatural and legends of myth. He tells the story of the sandwich maker; a being who is gifted magic to create sandwiches, who eats them and wields ultimate power upon good or evil.

The group understand what Athol said now and the group think it could be the Devil or someone that they know, who keeps it a secret and they will find out who did it!

Chapter 10

The Mystery Van

James told the police that "I'm gonna find my own detectives i've had enough of you all" Because the police won't do anything or try to do nothing. James decided to get some detectives so he rang up everyone so he found someone and the detectives said they be there a soon as possible.

"What's your name"? Bob i heard a big bang when i was on my jog in the pitch black and the water was clearer".

Sarah tells james that she heard a load bang when she was fishing, so she went over there and looked and it was a hut That fell from the sky.

James asks Tim to get back here, then he comes back because he wants To know more information about what's going on then he can investigate into it.

Chapter 11

New Rivals

James sees Jimmy in the hut and Jimmy is just standing there in the dark. Next minute James turns the light on and Jimmy is there looking at a sandwich on a table in front of him and they both stop and see

what this sandwich is doing on the table
They notice that it's a different colour on
it so it's not only a normal sandwich.

James asks jimmy what are you doing
here but Jimmy never responds back to
him, he just stare at him but James knows
that something's going on.

James is knowing something because Jimmy
has got that creepy grin on his face and
James recans that Jimmy knows where Bella
mum is hiding and he knows that he might
can get it out of Jimmy.

James feels uncomfortable because Jimmy
can get into his head that's why he feels
cold. james gets into his head.

Jimmy walks out of the hutt and disap-
pears back into hell in the mist of steam.

Chapter 12

Hearing Voices

```
Location:XXX

Time:
```

Jimmy started to walk away from the sandwich and started to go back to hell. Jimmy went back into hell and he planning to send voices out to the guardians and to tell them lies so the devil can have the sandwich. Jimmy started to send out the voice to the guardians to trick them.

Jimmy sent the ghost out so the message can be passed on. Jimmy be so happy if this goes to plan because it would trick the guardians and Jimmy would have the sandwich. The ghost took the message to give it to John, Athol, Davide, Bella, Ms Evans. The Devil started to give his evil smile to his lesser devils and he started laughing hard.

Jimmy started to send out the message to the guardians and it sent a horrible shock to the guardians and gave them goosebumps. The Great Devil sent out shivers down the guardians spines and the guardians started to get dizzy and started to get really scared of the voice inside their heads.

Some of the guardians have got the voice inside their heads and some of them don't listen to it because it's not true. The guardians were saying.If we listen more they might convince us to eat that sandwich and I think whoever sending these thoughts to our heads really want us to believe it!"

The devil who sent the thoughts to the guardians said to them "If you eat the sandwich nothing bad will happen and everyone will have a happy life". The guardians thinks it's a lie and trying to trick us so he can take us down in hell and keep us there so if we eat this sandwich we will go down in hell and something bad will definteley happen.

Chapter 13

A Friendly Conversation

Location:XXX

Time:

Davide stepped into his Mercedes Benz

AGM and began traveling down the motorway to Manchester Airport which is about 1hr 20 mins from now. Davide arrived back into his old town then people saw his Mercedes turn up and when he came out of his car and sees his face they were shocked to see him back in town Davide smiled after being welcomed back.

Davide rushed towards the in search of Bella and suddenly he bumps into a stranger, Davide apologise to him and said he was sorry and accepts his apologie.

Davide introduce himself to the stranger and chatting to each other whilst walking through town. Davide explains about a blackout that happened here from too days back and remembered hearing it on the news, so I made my way down as quickly as i could knowing the safety of my daugh-

ter which he hasn't seen for 5 years. The
stranger asked why he leave her in the first
place? Davide was because of a terrible
trauma to do with his wife's disappear-
ance, which the police stated murder and
that he couldn't stay here any longer bar-
ing his pain of being and the fact he's broke
os there was no supporting him and Bella
at the time.

Davide hopes that she forgives him for
leaving her so long ago and finds it in her
heart to let him become a dad once more
and to have the life could have together.

Chapter 14

Uncertain Truth

Location: Bella's house

Time: late morning

Bella starts her day off as a normal day being relaxed chilling in the sun on her front lawn, after a few minutes she hears the TV on for some strange reason. She goes in the house and turns off the TV. She went to get a drink from the kitchen and it turns on again and again and at this point she was getting frustrated and confused on why the TV kept turning on. She has a flashback of the time she has to ring the cops about her mum going missing. That day was a cloudy, windy and sunny Saturday late morning /afternoon, really hard for Bella because her mum went missing at 12:45 pm. Now she realised that she has to call police again but it's for the reason about what's she heard on the news about this certain sandwich and the shack. The voices said to her "Call the police, or we hurt your mum and we're not joking with that because we will make her tell us this special sandwich recipe. Also if you carry on to ignore our voices inside your head we will kill your mum and feed her to the souls." After Bella heard the voices she just carried on making her way to telling the police everything that she knows about this certain sandwich, her mum gave her a present. It was the special recipe to how make this sandwich. Bella runs to the phone whilst she heard the voices in her head but as soon as she got to the phone but something is stopping her from calling the police but she doesn't know what's stopping her from speaking to the police about the sandwich. After speaking to the police Bella decides to go with the police officers to the scene of the crime and she sees if she knows anything at the site of the where the shack and Bella and James arrive at the scene. Ms Evans and John got there first and Ms Evans starts to ask Bella some questions and some personal information about her and her mother and Johns sees a little bit of an connection with it all and john says " Ms Evans I've found something really interesting and you need to see this." Bella walks back to the car so she can be out of the way and let the police officers and the detectives do there job.

Whilst everyone was being nosey at the scene and wondering what's happening John and Ms Evans are trying to piece the puzzle together with the information that they have already and then out of the blue John hears his phone rings and he answer saying "hello this is detective John how I would be of assistance ? ", Then Bella replies saying " erm.. Hi it's Bella, im calling you

64

to tell you that i have some more information about the sandwich that you could be interested in ?". After he has heard the news, he starts to jump for joy because he's so happy like little puppies wagging their tails . Before John ends the call they make arrangement for them to meet up so Bella can tells them more information about the sandwich, then he's ends the call .

Rock tries to stop Bella from going out of the front door because the rock is making it hard for Bella to get to the police, Bella can't see the Rock but fell the presence of him and he doesn't want Bella to tell the police about him and Jimmy. Bella runs to the door and rushes to get to the cops but something stops her and as picks up the keys and heads towards the door and as about to the door handle but she's unable to open the door because the rock pulls her away from the door, then she fights back and finally she gets through the door then quickly runs to car and she panics and burst into tears, then she drives to meet up with cops .

Bella manages to get to police but is still hearing Rocks voices inside of her head but she's strong enough to block the voices out and tells the truth to the cops . Jimmy punishes Rock for failing to stop bella to go to the police . Jimmy hits Rock for failing him and but Bella's mum was there to see that happen and so was james but the great Devil made Rock move the prisoners to another room and so the Great Devil and Rock could have some words after the Rock moves them to another room he went back to the devil but they didn't know that James and Bella's mum know that were listening to the conversation and they were laughing because they had kidnap the police officer and Bella's mum in hell . The next day in hell the Great Devil and the Rock wants to talk to the prisoners and that's when they decide for only one of them to go back to earth and in some way they knew which one would go back roughly and who would stay, so they went and the Great Devil said " only one of you can go back to stinky earth but the other will have stay for eternity". Bella's mum remembered that she spoke to Ms Evans before she went missing and she said to Ms Evans " When this day comes please can you talk to Bella in secret so your other colleagues don't know what your doing."

Chapter 15

The Fight Begins

```
Location:XXX

Time:
```

James creeps into the hut and looks around and spots a sandwich on the table. James is thinking "Why is there a strange sandwich on the table?" He finds something strange and unusual on the sandwich but he doesn't know yet what it might be.

James finds the devil in the hut but the devil has never been questioned, and certainly not by a human before so James is weary of what he's got to say to the him.

Jimmy starts getting agitated over James' questioning; he is crossing his arms looking at him angrily and look liking he's going beat him up.

Jimmy and James get into a massive fight with each other because Jimmy got really angry over James questioning; there was nobody around to stop them from fighting.

Rock comes out of the hell and pulls James into a dark hole and James is wondering why is he in a dark hole. Why cant he see anything?

Rock has gone dark black and James doesn't know where he's gone. He is falling down to hell. He's hearing the blood curdling screaming of people being kept in the dark, warm land of hell.

Chapter 16

Freedom Of Rights

```
Location:XXX

Time:
```

The town people in the town had a meeting about the blackout what happened in the lake in the town. Bella got the meeting started and discussed about they want answers from the police and the town people are not happy.The town people including Bella, Athol, Davide, John then all of them including the towns people but Ms evans decided to not to go because Ms Evans goes back to HQ instead of joining the mob.

Bella lead the mob through the town and about to use violence to people who are trying to stop them. The shops around the town had to shut down because the shop might get damage with the violence and fighting with the town people. The people started to hide from the mob because they got scared and frightened when the people started using violence.

Bella and the mob eventually arrived at the lake with anger and violence and frustration with the police. The mob started fighting and demolishing stuff around the lake so they can get attention to the police so they get answers from them. The mob carried on using violence around the lake and making lots of mess and trying to tell the police what they want.

Ahol stands up to the mob and try to tell them there's a devil there and he tried and tried. Ahol said to the mob it's too dangers to find him he is powerful and he could hurt us really bad and try to kill us and send us down in hell. The people was thinking about it and talking about it together.

The town people who was in the mob were saying he was old and wise so they started talking and talking. Ahol decided to leave the area of the lake and the mob decided to do the same and calm down and walk away from the lake and go back to do normally stuff. The shops open backup and running and everyone back to work where they normally go.

Chapter 17

It's Only Just Begun

```
Location:XXX

Time:
```

Jimmy is in hell forming a big army to

face Bella and her guardians. Jimmy is lining up a load of army people for when they attack them. Jimmy started to talking to his army and telling them what they have to do and not to do and to do the right thing.

Meanwhile bella is gathering up the guardians and getting ready to start the war and she ask Davide if he wanted he join and he said "yes, but we don't know who Davide is, so would he fight Jimmy and his army?"

Ms Evans most probably would have said no to Bella because she didn't want to get involved with a devil who can mess with people heads that's why she said no to Bella. Then she was going back to her HQ not to be parted ways a couple of minutes later.

Later on, James comes and tries to rescue Bella's Mum but there is a powerful demon in the way so James has to try to get past Rock to rescue the Mother, but Rock is too strong to get through but how is James going get Bella's Mother out of the hell?

Bella is planning to separate the army by getting them to distract the devils while they try to get out of hell but the plan doesn't work because one of the devil's finds them trying to escape, so they all get back together. Bella had no choice but to fight them all until they were able to get out of hell but there was one person who they couldn't get past, and that was Rock because he was the strongest one there.

Chapter 18

The Great Sacrifice: Part 2

Location:XXX

Time:

Great Devil says " only one of you can

go through the portail and the one other has to stay in hell with me for a bit ".

James and Adele knew that only one of them can go back and James says

" You go because you have family back on earth and I've done my time and I don't think that I can go back to the station because my boss wants more and more information on the lake and i don't think that i can give it to him. "

Adele tries to say something but James won't let her because he knows that he is making the right (choice and in some way it's not the best choice that's he's made) but the police officer knows that Adele's family are missing her so much. They would like to come back home safe and sound and the Devils are making them hurrying up with their choice on who stays and who's goes and Adele and James are ready to say on who's going and who is staying in hell, james says to the (the Great Devil)

" I am sacrificing myself for Adele to go back to earth and I am going to stay here with you if you will accept me?"

Rock says to great devil " it's time to go to battle and do you want me to stay with the victim to make sure that he doesn't move ¿'.

The Great Devil says to his army It's time to battle and we are doing to win no matter what because i want to show earth what we are made of and if we win, we will turn earth into hell and everyone will have to bow down to me and also i want to give them a taste of their own medicine!!!!!!!!!!!!!!!

Rocks interrupts the Great Devil saying

" what happens if we lose and all of hell be killed and destroyed, do you want that your mighty king?" After a while the army heads towards earth to start the battle but they bring James as the prisoner so the town may act a little different if they see what the rock does to James .

After a while the army heads towards earth to start the battle but they bring James as the prisoner so the town may act a little different if they see what the rock does to James. As soon as they get to Earth everyone starts to think and talks about why we should battle with the gods from hell ? because they see james hurt and injured from the metal chains from his ankles, and scares on the face and the body.

Chapter 19

The Guardians
Of The Sandwich

Location:XXX

Time:

After the curse was broken, now the last

sandwich was eaten the shack is destroyed closing the gate between hell and Earth. it finally ended the prophecy with it's chaos upon the town and the world. Most of the town was buried in earth and rubble because the gate being broken and the barrier reformed made an intense earthquake, but in a miracle the population survived.

After stopping Jimmy with the sandwich, it's powers sent all the demons back to the underworld. Bella and her mother are reunited once more. With the knowledge she gained Bella must use her gift to make another one in its place to recreate the chant and form a group of worthy guardians to watch over and protect the new sandwich. Excitingly she has great friends who fought hard along her side against monsters, so she thought to herself "Why would I need to search for them since my friends are the most worthy team ever?"

Athol feeling relief turns to everyone saying "Thank you for putting an end to evil forces and becoming the ones who are worthy of protecting the good in this world". Realising what they can do and what they've accomplished now pledge allegiance until one day they'll join forces as one to vanquish evil whenever it returns.

For now, they go their separate ways living to the fullest, Bella has the family she wanted for so long and together her father and mother explore the world whilst practicing their powers as mother and daughter.

Since James has given his life during the outbreak the police department and squadron hold a funeral in his honour Ms

Evans took a moment of silence as well. After that day she stayed in town for a while and left for retirement finding another lead in life.

As for Athol, well he finally opened himself to the town and became the town's counsellr and provider to the school and hospital, he is now everyone's hero and lives his life in peace.

When days go past and time runs slow never forget that if you even feel like danger is close, or some ancient evil tries showing itself to the world, don't forget that your future is protected by the greatest team of legends to come. "Guardians of the cursed sandwich".

THE END

Our Authors

Alice Broad

Alice has worked really well during the workshop, often outside of her comfort zone, and on topics with which she is unfamiliar. Alice created one of the central characters; Bella', the young woman entrusted with a dark and dangerous secret.

Joe Hill

Joe created the character of James', the ex-military detective, who is determined to find out what is going on in his town. Joe also worked on the illustrations to accompany the story, demonstrating his fantastic artistic skills and creativity.

Ashley Pattison

Ashley worked really well to keep a track of the chapters and word count on behalf of the group. He challenged himself daily to try and write more than the day before! He created the character of Davide, a man traumatised by a devastating family event.

Kyran Phokeerdoss

Kyran enjoyed developing his character's back story and the world' in which the book is set, coming up with many of the central themes. Kyran created the character of Athol, an unusual outsider who arouses suspicion amongst his neighbours.

Mitchell Powell

Mitchell (writing more than we have EVER know him to before!) created the amazingly dark and demonic world addressed in the novel. He used imagery and descriptive language to make a truly frightening other dimension.

Morgan Warrilow

Morgan added a different perspective to the story, creating the shape-shifting character of Rock. His character forms a link between two alternative worlds, which we find out in the story. He developed his editing skills, ensuring that work was corrected and made sense.

Jordan White

Jordan created the character of John, a detective from out of town. Jordan really developed both his writing and editing skills during the week, also working with others to proofread and improve on individual chapters..

Emma Williams

Emma worked both individually and collaboratively with other members of the group to develop the character of Ms. Evans, and also the detectives working with her character. She also supported others within the group if they needed any help.